To Ursula Barnett,
for her encouragement and wonderful friendship – L.B.

For my mum – every brushstroke – K.L.

About Sieta and Satara

Qolweni Township is just outside the holiday village
of Plettenberg Bay on the Western Cape of South Africa.
Many children live there and the people care
for them just as they cared for Sieta. Just up the road
is the Knysna Elephant Park. A real baby elephant used
to live there, and his name was Satara.

Home Now copyright © Frances Lincoln Limited 2006
Text copyright © Lesley Beake 2006
Illustrations copyright © Karin Littlewood 2006
The right of Karin Littlewood to be identified as the illustrator of this work has been asserted
by her in accordance with the Copyright, Designs and Patents Act, 1988 (United Kingdom).

First published in Great Britain in 2006 by
Frances Lincoln Children's Books, 4 Torriano Mews
Torriano Avenue, London NW5 2RZ
www.franceslincoln.com

British Library Cataloguing in Publication Data
available on request

ISBN 1-84507-105-0

Set in Usherwood

Printed in China

1 3 5 7 9 8 6 4 2

Home Now

Lesley Beake

Illustrated by Karin Littlewood

FRANCES LINCOLN CHILDREN'S BOOKS

Sieta lay in her bed looking up at the black
plastic roof of her new home.

"This isn't my real home," she thought. "My real home
is over the mountains."

But this was home now. Everybody said so.

"This is your home now, Sieta," they said. "We'll look
after you and keep you safe." And she did feel safe.

But it wasn't her real home.

Sieta stared into the black. There were pictures
up there in the black, pictures she remembered
from her other life over the mountains.

Sieta remembered a green garden in a dry land.
Two tins of geraniums stood outside the front door,
one pink and one red. Ma loved those geraniums.
Every evening, after Ma and Pa and Sieta had washed,
they carried their wash-basins to water the flowers
and vegetables.

Sieta remembered when she and Ma and Pa
went to church on Sundays, all in their Sunday best.
That was her favourite picture.

But sometimes the other pictures came,
the sad ones. Then Sieta would shut
her eyes, squeezing them tight to try
to stop the sadness.

Sieta saw her mother getting sicker…
and thinner… and quieter, and her father
getting gentler and softer and sadder.
One day they were just not there any more.
Sieta saw women bringing her plates of food,
hugging her and crying into her hair. She saw old people
coming with soft pink roses for her, and children hanging
round the gate and not knowing what to say.
Then she saw Aunty coming on the bus to bring Sieta
to Home Now – and now Sieta lived with Aunty.

Home Now was a busy place. People were building
new houses and new lives. Sieta watched them.

Home Now was a friendly place. People smiled
at Sieta. Sieta didn't smile back. She just looked
and looked at the pictures in her head.

Sieta went to school with the other children,
just down the dirt road from Home Now.
One day, Sieta's teacher took the children
to the elephant park.

"These are orphan elephants," said the lady
at the park. "They come from Kruger National Park.
They have lost their families and are staying here
with us, where they are safe."

"Just like me," thought Sieta. "This is their
Home Now."

"And this," said the lady, "is our smallest
elephant. His name is Satara."

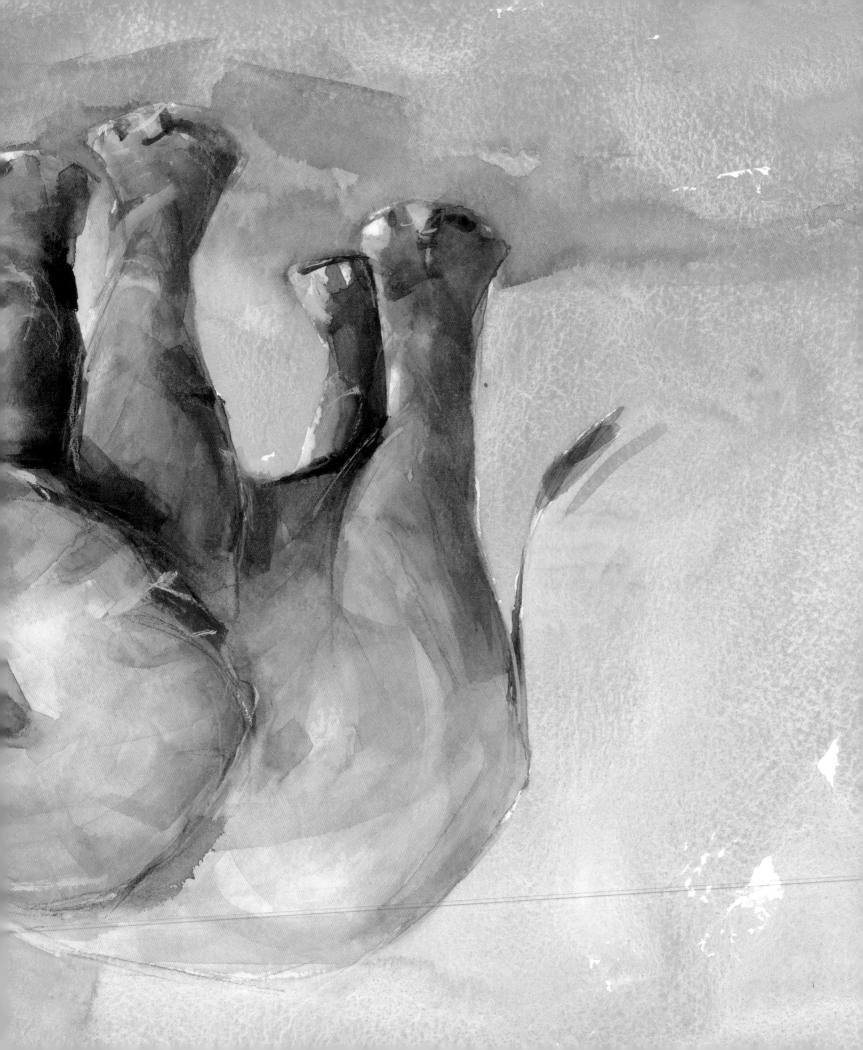

Sieta held her breath. She stared
and stared at the baby elephant.
Satara was beautiful. His skin was grey
and wrinkled and it didn't quite fit him,
as if it was two sizes too big for him.
His eyes were small and wise.
The lady from the elephant park was
speaking to Sieta. Her voice seemed
to come from a long way away.
"Would you like to touch him?"
she asked.

Sieta took two steps forward. Slowly she reached out her hand and touched Satara. His skin was leathery and rough. Sieta smelled his elephant smell and it smelled like wild places far, far away.

Slowly, the baby elephant lifted his trunk.
He looked straight at Sieta. Sieta looked at him.
That night, there was a new picture behind
Sieta's eyes – a picture of the baby elephant.

Next day, Sieta was still thinking about Satara.
After school, when the other children ran ahead
on the dirt road back to Home Now, she hung back.
   Then her feet turned on to the road that led
to the elephants.

The lady at the elephant park did not look
surprised to see Sieta.

"Have you come to see Satara?" she asked.

"I think he might be waiting for you."

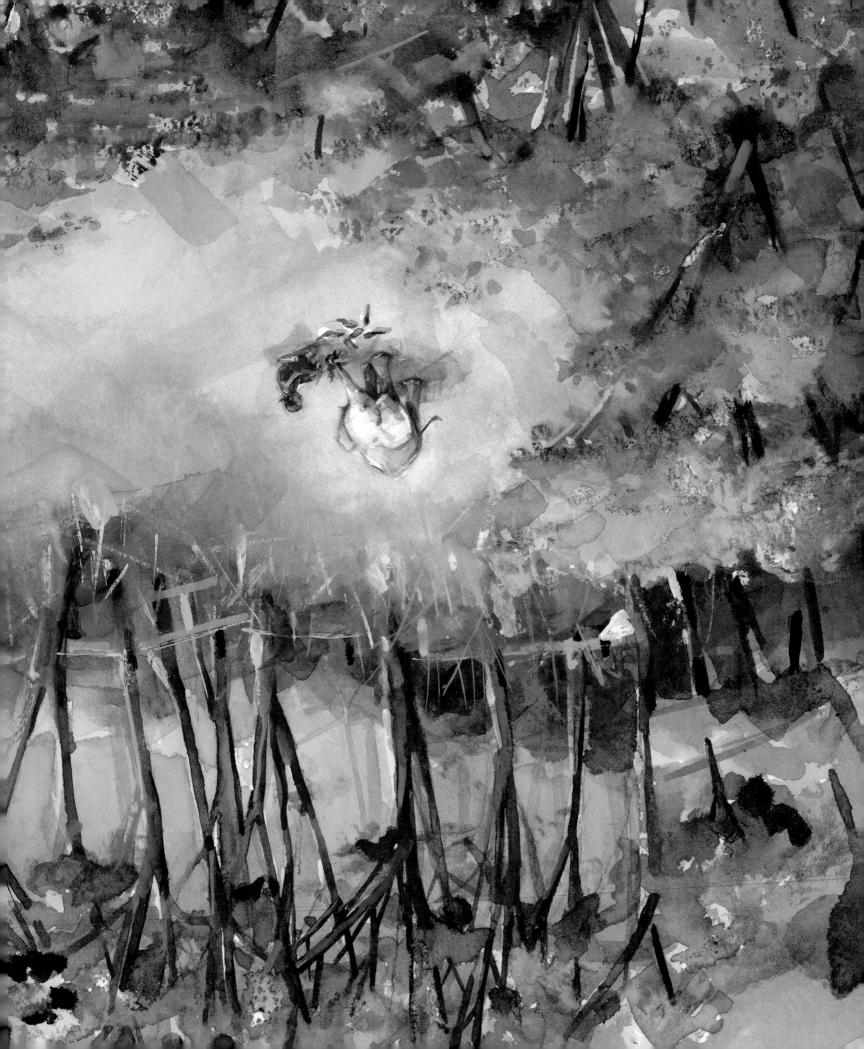

Satara was eating some leaves in a place on his own.
The big elephants had gone to walk in the forest with
their trainer, but Satara was too small to go walking.
He munched his leaves, picking them up carefully
with his small trunk and stuffing them into his mouth.
While he ate, he looked at Sieta, and she looked at him.
    Sieta listened to the sound of the munching baby
elephant and the wind stirring the leaves in the trees.

Sieta's thoughts went far away. She saw a picture
in her mind of great, grey elephants walking through
the forest with one small elephant walking behind.
She saw Satara with his family in the faraway land
where he was born.

And then the soft sounds of the big elephants
coming home brought her back from her dream.

The next morning, Sieta watched the people of Home Now cutting wood, bringing water, making fires, cooking, finding and making things for their homes, looking after babies, children and parents, looking after each other.

They were not always happy. Sometimes they were sad.
Sometimes they were afraid. But they laughed and sang.
They danced and played soccer. They were strong.

Then one of the children ran over and asked Sieta to play.

Afterwards, Sieta walked back to Aunty's.
Aunty was putting two tins of geraniums
outside the front door, one pink and one red.
   "Hello, Auntie!" said Sieta.
Auntie held out her arms.
Sieta hugged her... and gave her a big smile.

A Note on the Story

Sieta's story is fictional, but her plight is a real one shared
by many children in Africa. Millions are orphans because one
or both of their parents have died of Acquired Immune
Deficiency Syndrome (AIDS).

AIDS is a disease that weakens the body's immune system.
People suffering from it become ill with other diseases and die,
especially if they do not have enough to eat. Medicines to slow
down the effects of AIDS are expensive and hard to get, so AIDS
is always worse for people who are poor – and many people
in Africa are very, very poor.

So many people have died that families and communities
are sometimes unable to cope and governments are overwhelmed
by the size of the problem. Orphaned children are often cared
for by grandparents or other family members – if there are any
left. In some cases children have to look after other children,
struggling with their own fears, unhappiness and poverty, battling
to survive.

Until a cure is found for AIDS, we need to find ways to prevent
adults from becoming infected, and to give treatment and care
to everyone affected by the epidemic. AIDS is not going to go
away. It is not something we can forget about. It is an enormous,
growing problem for everyone – and especially for the children
of Africa who are most at risk.